A Deer Visits Nubble Lighthouse

The true story about
a deer at Sohier Park
in Cape Neddick, Maine

Written and Illustrated by
Denise F. Brown
Edited by Crystal Ward Kent

A Deer Visits Nubble Lighthouse
ISBN-10:
0985263938
ISBN-13:
978-0-9852639-3-5

www.deervisitsNubble.com
www.raccoonstudios.com
Raccoon Studios, 692 Sagamore Avenue, Portsmouth, NH 03801 USA 603-436-0788

About the author/illustrator

     The author and illustrator, Denise F. Brown of Portsmouth, New Hampshire has produced several
children's books.
     Brown, along with husband, John O'Sullivan, is the co-owner of Ad-Cetera Graphics and
Raccoon Studios of Portsmouth. She is the author/illustrator of *Wind: Wild Horse Rescue* adventure book
and is well known throughout the region for her stunning watercolors of Seacoast scenes, architectural
renderings, horse illustrations, and her pony figurine designs with The Trail of Painted Ponies. She is
also the creator of the popular series of children's coloring books, *Ted Gets Out,* which celebrates the
adventures of one of her cats, and her mini children's book, *Abenaki, the Indian Pony* about a little horse
who travels across the country. She illustrated *Tugboat River Rescue,* by Crystal Ward Kent.
See her artwork at www.raccoonstudios.com, www.tugboatrescue.com and www.windwildhorse.com.

The small herd of deer moved quietly
through the Maine forest. Lily, a small doe,
and her family, had been grazing among the
thickets and low shrubs.

It was a bright winter day.
The ocean was nearby, sparkling in the sun.
Lily loved the fresh salt air and the roar of the surf.
Although it was windy, the sun was warm on her thick
winter coat and she was not a bit cold.

Lily and her family began wandering through the yards of the little beach houses with their tidy, white picket fences. Because it was winter, no one was around. All the summer families were far away. The deer ate whatever bits of grass and shrubbery they could find.

Soon, they stopped near the beach with a view of Nubble Lighthouse. The lighthouse, which stands on a rocky island close to shore, is quite famous. It is very old (built in 1879) and people stop to photograph it all the time — even in winter. Although the lighthouse seemed close by, it was difficult to reach. People usually had to go over by boat.

Every morning, Lily looked at the island and wondered how sweet the grasses might be over there. Her parents told her to never go there because it was too dangerous.

A deer would have to swim to get there and the ocean currents between the mainland and the island were very strong and unpredictable.

8

On this sunny morning, the tide was low and many rocks were visible beneath the water. To Lily's eyes, it almost looked like there was a path to the island — even though the water was still two or three feet deep.

"I bet I can wade through the water and get to the island today!" thought Lily.

NO TRESPASSING ON ISLAND
TOWN OF YORK

The more she thought about it,
the more she liked the idea.

To her family's surprise, she jumped
into the cold water with a splash. She swam
the short distance to the rocky shore and then
scrambled up the rocks to the grass-covered
hillside with its light dusting of snow.

"I made it!" she bleated to her family.
They looked scared watching her.

Her father bellowed, "Please be careful on those rocks!
Come back to the shore right now!"

NO
TRESPASSING
ON ISLAND
TOWN OF YORK

14

But Lily ignored her father's warning. "I'm okay! I am going to explore the island for a little while!"

15

And with that, she began leaping in the air and running around the hill. Besides the lighthouse, the island had a small lighthouse keeper's cottage and some outbuildings.

She jumped the fences around the house and laughed to herself, "How much fun this is!"

As she was playing and exploring, she did not realize that the tide
had started to come back in. The water between the island
and the shore was rising higher and higher.
Her family watched and waited for her to come back, but still she
played. They saw how high the ocean was becoming. Lily's "path"
was disappearing and the waves were getting bigger, too!

"Lily!" cried her mother, "You must wait on the island until the tide goes out again and the water is lower! It is too dangerous for you to come back now!" Her mother looked carefully around, and then added, "We have to leave now, before people start walking along the beach and see us."

"We are going back to the woods and will watch for you to cross tomorrow morning!" said her father. "Remember, do not try to swim until the tide is low! If you huddle down behind a rock or shrub, no one will see you and you will be safe."

NO
TRESPASSING
ON ISLAND
TOWN OF YORK

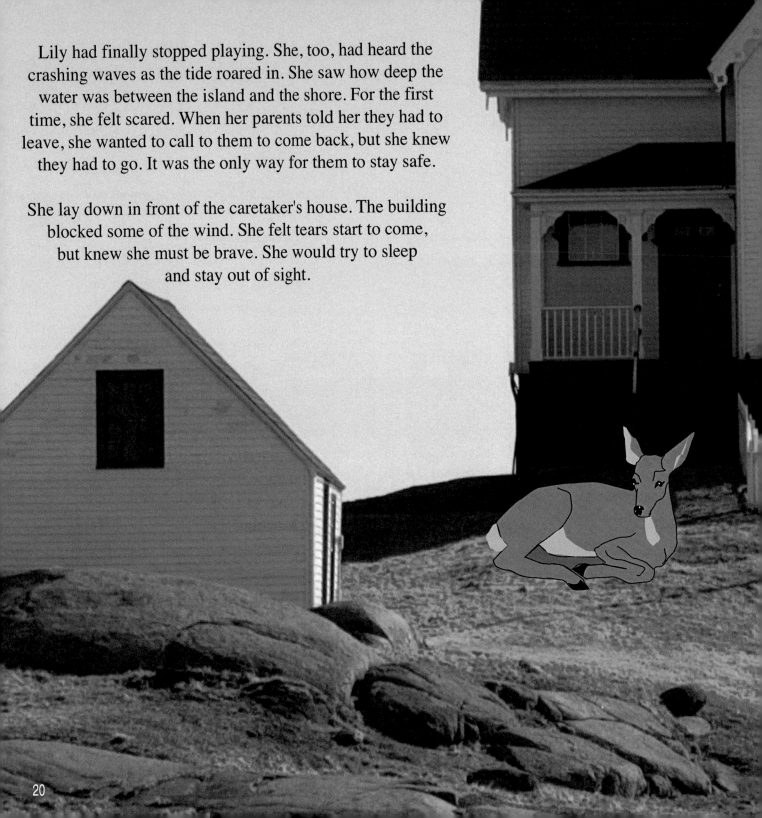

Lily had finally stopped playing. She, too, had heard the crashing waves as the tide roared in. She saw how deep the water was between the island and the shore. For the first time, she felt scared. When her parents told her they had to leave, she wanted to call to them to come back, but she knew they had to go. It was the only way for them to stay safe.

She lay down in front of the caretaker's house. The building blocked some of the wind. She felt tears start to come, but knew she must be brave. She would try to sleep and stay out of sight.

Trying to hide was difficult. The island had no trees, and only a few spindly shrubs. There was very little to eat and nothing but salt water to drink.

Lily was getting hungry and thirsty.
She decided to walk around a bit and see if
there was any snow left on the island.
Eating the snow would ease her thirst.

Suddenly, she saw them — people! They were on the shore,
pointing at HER and taking pictures with their cameras.
She had been spotted!

She could hear them saying,
"Look! There is a deer
on Nubble Light!"

24

People were sending pictures and emails telling their friends about her. More people came and were walking all over the rocks trying to get a glimpse of the little deer on Nubble Island.

The wind was blowing and it was very cold standing outside on the rocks, but the people did not leave. They wanted to see if the deer would jump into the water.

Soon the newspapers sent reporters to investigate what was happening.

Lily started to panic. "I must hide!" she thought.
She stumbled over rocks and ice, trying to get
out of sight. The wind howled and the
waves beat upon the rocks.
The gulls soaring overhead cried out sadly,
"You are alone; you are alone;
on an island, all alone."

Tired, she ducked behind a small red shed. The sun
was going down and the wind was getting colder.

It had been a long and scary day.
As it got dark, the people watching her finally
went away. Lily felt calmer after they left. She
tried to sleep, but the red light of the lighthouse
kept flashing all night long, waking her up.

Lily looked at the sky. She saw millions of
twinkling stars and even a shooting star.
She knew the same moon and stars
gleamed above her parents deep in the woods.
Gradually, she nodded off to
sleep, dreaming she was with them.

The next morning, she was surprised to see even
more people on the beach. A big crowd was watching her.
With so many people there, Lily was afraid
to cross back to the mainland.

Because of the crowds, Lily's family was nowhere to be found. She knew they must be worried. Would she ever be able to get home?

Just then, Lily spotted
two people wading
across to the island.
They were Parks and
Recreation employees.
She did not know it,
but they hoped
to rescue her.

NO
TRESPASSING
ON ISLAND

TOWN OF YORK

Instead, the sight of them panicked Lily.
She must escape! She ran past the caretaker's house.
She leaped over the picket fence and ran around the outbuildings.
Then she raced past the lighthouse.
There was nowhere to go and nowhere to hide,
and the men were getting closer!

The men were talking. "She looks healthy, but very young," said one. "I guess she is just a curious doe who wanted to visit the island," said the other.

Just then, Lily sprinted for the water.
It was sink or swim she thought!

37

Lily scampered down the cliff like a mountain goat,
made a big leap into the deep water, and started to swim.

The crowd gasped. They feared she would get caught
in the strong currents or pummeled by the waves and drown.
If she did not get out of the cold water soon,
she could freeze to death.

Lily swam as hard and fast as she could around the island
to a place where she thought she could make land.
Big sharp boulders and slippery
rocks were everywhere, and all the while,
huge waves crashed in between them.

But Lily was a strong swimmer. Her thick coat protected her from the cold water.
Within minutes, she reached a rocky point between Sohier Park and Short Sands Beach.
She practically flew out of the waves as she reached shore.

People cheered as she reached the beach.

Once her hooves touched land, so fast did she run that nobody
saw where she went. She raced past the beach houses and
through backyards, leaping fences as she ran.
Finally, she was past the town and into the woods.

It did not take long for her to find her family. They were hiding in the
thickets near a tiny pond. They had seen Lily jump into the ocean.
When they heard the people holler they were scared,
but were glad she was free from her island prison.
Now, here she was, safe with them.

Little by little, the people went home. But the story of the deer on the island, and her dramatic escape, was on all the television stations and in every local newspaper. Lily had no idea she was famous.

She was just glad to be home. "I will never cross the ocean again!" she told her parents. "There was not even any good grass to eat over there!"

The family drifted deeper into the woods. They would return to eat the sweet grasses near the beach another day, and always remember Lily's escape from the island.

The End.

Author's Note: Nubble Light's official name is Cape Neddick Light as it is located in Cape Neddick, Maine. Captain John Smith gave it its nickname because he said it stood on a "nubble of land." Nubble Light is one of the most photographed lighthouses in the country. It is still a working lighthouse, but is now fully automated. It is owned by the Town of York and managed by the Friends of Nubble Light.

Denise F. Brown

Special thanks to

Crystal Ward Kent of Eliot, Maine
for helping edit this book
Kent owns Kent Creative, a creative services
agency providing writing, design, marketing and
PR out of Dover, New Hampshire.

and

Laura Brown
for helping to proofread my books

More books Denise Brown
has worked on
Visit www.raccoonstudios.com

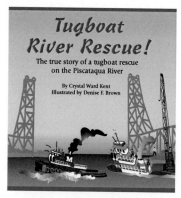

"Tugboat River Rescue"
children's book
written by Crystal Ward Kent
illustrated by Denise F. Brown
www.tugboatrescue.com

"Wind, Wild Horse Rescue"
about the plight of mustangs today
written and illustrated by
Denise F. Brown
www.windwildhorse.com
ages 9 to adult

"Ted the Cat"
Children's Coloring Books
illustrated by
Denise F. Brown
edited by
John F. O'Sullivan
www.raccoonstudios.com

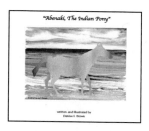

"Abenaki the Indian Pony"
a mini children's book
written and Illustrated by
Denise F. Brown
artist for The Trail of Painted Ponies
www.raccoonstudios.com

Made in the USA
Middletown, DE
04 April 2015